KING ARTHUR
The Sword in the Stone

TALES OF KING ARTHUR

KING
ARThUR
The Sword
in the Stone

written and illustrated by
HUDSON TALBOTT

Books of Wonder · Morrow Junior Books · New York

Watercolors were used for the full-color art.
The text type is 15 point Goudy Old Style.

Printed in the United States of America.
1   2   3   4   5   6   7   8   9   10

Library of Congress Cataloging-in-Publication Data
Talbott, Hudson.
King Arthur—the sword in the stone / Hudson Talbott.
p.   cm.
Summary: The only person able to draw a sword from an
anvil, a young boy proves himself to be the
successor to the throne of all Britain.
ISBN 0-688-09403-1. —ISBN 0-688-09404-X (lib. bdg.)
1. Arthurian romances. 2. Arthur, King. [1. Knights and
knighthood—Folklore. 2. Folklore—England.] I. Title.
PZ8.1.T133Sw   1991   398.2—dcE —dc20   90-28104   CIP   AC

Books of Wonder is a registered trademark of Ozma, Inc.

For my father

In ancient times, when Britain was still a wild and restless place, there lived a noble king named Uther. After many years of turmoil, Uther defeated the invading barbarians and drove them from the land. For this triumph, his fellow British lords proclaimed him their high king, or Pendragon, meaning "Dragon's Head."

Soon after his coronation, Uther-Pendragon met and fell in love with the beautiful Lady Igraine, a widow whose husband he had killed in battle. He married her and adopted her two young daughters, Margaise and Morgan le Fay. The price for this love was a high one, however. In his passion, the king had asked for the help of his sorcerer, Merlin, in winning the hand of Lady Igraine. In return he had agreed to give up their firstborn son. Merlin had foreseen great evil descending upon the king and felt that he alone could protect a young heir in the dangerous times ahead.

Before long, a beautiful boy-child was born. But the joy surrounding the birth was brief, for Merlin soon appeared to take the child away.

"But the child was just born!" exclaimed Uther. "How did you find out so quickly?"

Silently, the old sorcerer led the king to a balcony and pointed upward. There overhead was a great dragon formed by the stars. Its vast wings arched over the countryside, and its tail swept north beyond the horizon. "You see by this sign, my lord, that it is not I who calls for your son, but destiny."

Sadly, the king gave up his son, for Merlin convinced him that the child's great future was threatened. Indeed, Uther-Pendragon died within a year from a traitor's poison and Britain was once again plunged into darkness.

After the death of the high king, the struggle for leadership tore Britain to pieces. The great alliance King Uther had forged was shattered into dozens of quarreling, petty kingdoms—leaving no united force to oppose foreign invasion. Barbarians swept in once again and order gave way to chaos. Marauding knights roamed the countryside, taking what they wanted and burning the rest. No one was safe at home, and travel was even more dangerous, with outlaws ruling the roads. Fear was a constant companion of those who managed to stay alive.

After sixteen turbulent years, the archbishop of Canterbury summoned Merlin to help restore order. Although the two men were of different faiths, they had great respect for each other and shared much wisdom between them.

"I am at a loss, Sir Wizard!" confided the archbishop. "I don't know how to help the people, and they are suffering more each day. If only Uther-Pendragon were here!"

"I share your concerns, my lord, but I have good news," said Merlin. "Although the end of King Uther's reign left us in the dark for many years, it is at last time for the sun to return to Britain. A brilliant sun, my lord. Perhaps the brightest that Britain will ever know."

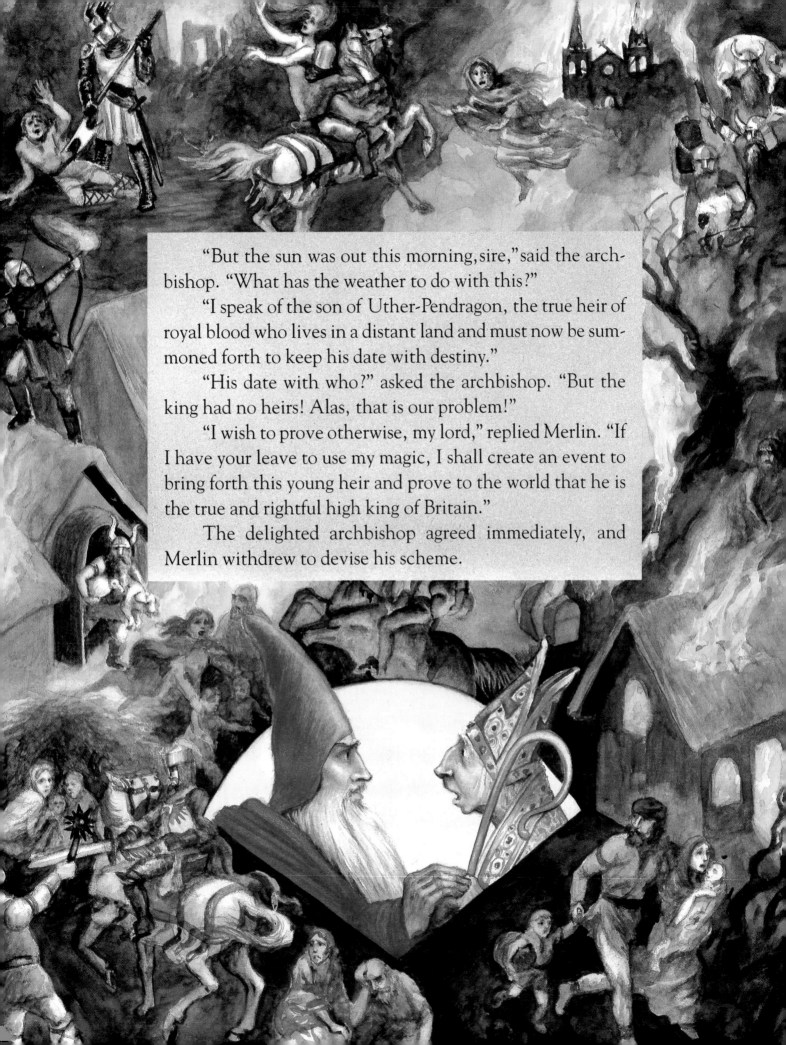

"But the sun was out this morning, sire," said the archbishop. "What has the weather to do with this?"

"I speak of the son of Uther-Pendragon, the true heir of royal blood who lives in a distant land and must now be summoned forth to keep his date with destiny."

"His date with who?" asked the archbishop. "But the king had no heirs! Alas, that is our problem!"

"I wish to prove otherwise, my lord," replied Merlin. "If I have your leave to use my magic, I shall create an event to bring forth this young heir and prove to the world that he is the true and rightful high king of Britain."

The delighted archbishop agreed immediately, and Merlin withdrew to devise his scheme.

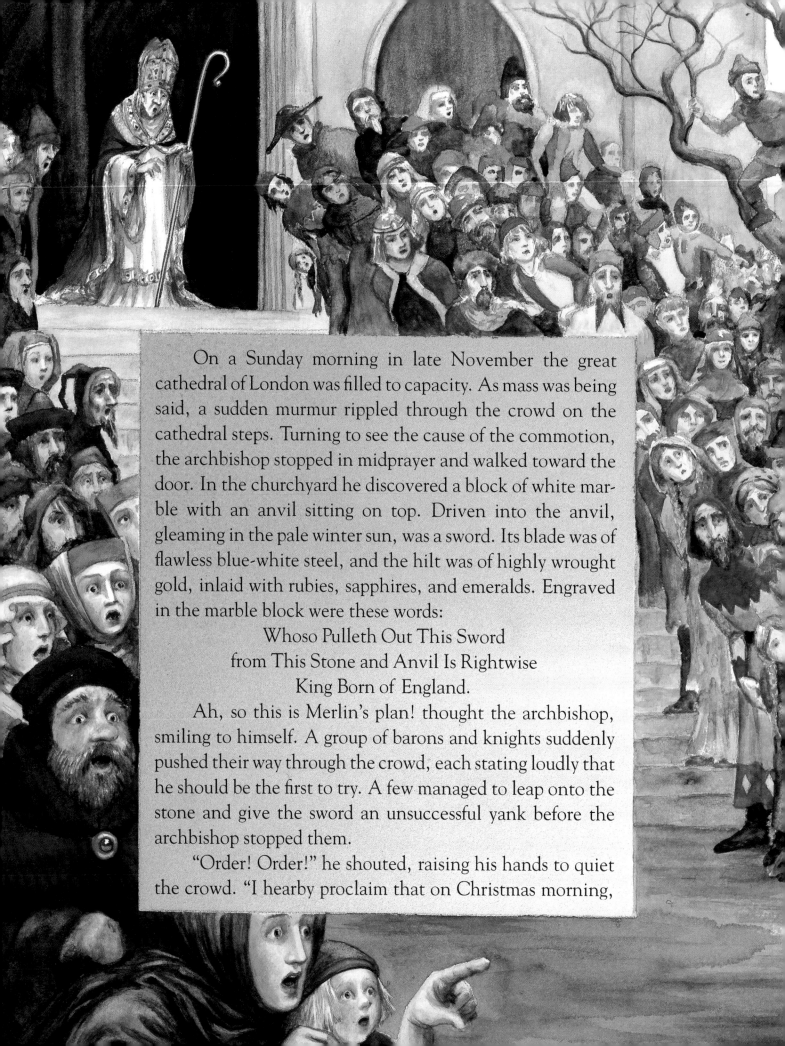

On a Sunday morning in late November the great cathedral of London was filled to capacity. As mass was being said, a sudden murmur rippled through the crowd on the cathedral steps. Turning to see the cause of the commotion, the archbishop stopped in midprayer and walked toward the door. In the churchyard he discovered a block of white marble with an anvil sitting on top. Driven into the anvil, gleaming in the pale winter sun, was a sword. Its blade was of flawless blue-white steel, and the hilt was of highly wrought gold, inlaid with rubies, sapphires, and emeralds. Engraved in the marble block were these words:

Whoso Pulleth Out This Sword
from This Stone and Anvil Is Rightwise
King Born of England.

Ah, so this is Merlin's plan! thought the archbishop, smiling to himself. A group of barons and knights suddenly pushed their way through the crowd, each stating loudly that he should be the first to try. A few managed to leap onto the stone and give the sword an unsuccessful yank before the archbishop stopped them.

"Order! Order!" he shouted, raising his hands to quiet the crowd. "I hearby proclaim that on Christmas morning,

one month from today, all those who consider themselves worthy of attempting to pull this sword from the stone and anvil will be given the opportunity. He who wins the sword, thereby wins the kingdom."

A mighty roar of approval rose from the crowd. Some even danced and stomped their feet. Noticing how pleased they were, the archbishop went further. "And to celebrate this momentous occasion, a tournament shall be held on Christmas Eve."

With this, the delighted parishioners swept the flustered archbishop onto their shoulders and carried him jubilantly around the stone several times before setting him down. They hadn't had such cause for celebration in a long, long time.

To all parts of the kingdom, messengers rushed out, carrying the archbishop's proclamation. Every castle and village was alerted, from Sussex to Cornwall and, finally, to the dark forest of Wales. There lived a certain gentle knight by the name of Sir Ector Bonmaison with his two sons. The elder was a handsome, robust youth, recently knighted and now known as Sir Kay. The younger was a gentle blond lad of about sixteen whom Sir Ector and his wife had adopted as an infant. His name was Arthur. Although Arthur was not of his blood, Sir Ector loved both sons equally and devoted himself to their upbringing.

Sir Kay was the first to hear the news of the great events in London, for as usual, he was in the courtyard polishing his helmet when the messenger arrived.

"A tournament! At last, a tournament!" he shouted. "We must set out for London at once! Father, you know what this means to me."

"Yes, son, I do," said Sir Ector, bringing the weary messenger a bowl of food. "I was young and hot-blooded once, too, and eager to show the world my worthiness of knighthood. But this sword-pulling contest—do you wish to be king, as well?" he asked Kay with a smile.

"I make no pretense about that, sir. To prove myself on the field of battle is *my* dream."

"Please remember that, my son," said Sir Ector. "Pursuing one's goals with integrity is all that matters. Now go find Arthur so that we may prepare to leave. London is a long way off."

Arthur had wandered off alone, as he often did after finishing his chores. He was as devoted as ever to being a good squire for his brother. But, after all, Kay was *Sir* Kay now, and he rarely had anything to say to his younger brother except to bark orders at him. Arthur didn't mind, though. He was happy just to watch Kay practice his jousting and to dream of someday riding beside him in battle. In the meantime, he had to content himself with his other companions—Lionel and Jasper, his dogs; Cosmo, his falcon; the orphaned fox cubs he kept hidden in the hollow log; and the deer that came to the edge of the woods when he whistled. He was in the woods now, patiently holding out a handful of oats for the deer, when Kay came bounding through the meadows to find him.

"Arthur, come quickly!" he shouted. "We're leaving for London at once! There's a big tournament. Here's your chance to show me what a good squire you can be! Hurry!"

Arthur stood silently for a moment. He had never been more than a few miles from his home. Was he daydreaming? Or was he really going to London to help Sir Kay bring honor and glory to their family as the whole world looked on? He ran back home, doubting his own ears until he reached the courtyard and saw Sir Ector preparing their horses for the journey.

All of Britain seemed to be making its way to London Town that Christmas. Kings and dukes, earls and barons, counts and countesses funneled into the city gates for the great contest. Sir Ector was pleased to see old friends and fellow knights. Sir Kay was eager to register for the jousting. And Arthur was simply dazzled by it all.

As Sir Ector and his sons made their way through the city streets, a glint of sunlight on steel caught Arthur's eye. How odd, he thought. A sword thrust point-first into an anvil on top of a block of marble, sitting in a churchyard— surrounded by guards! London is so full of wonders!

Dawn arrived with a blare of trumpets, calling all contestants to the tournament. In Sir Ector's tent, Arthur buckled the chain mail onto Sir Kay and slipped the tunic of the Bonmaison colors over his brother's head. Sir Ector stood and watched until the preparation was complete and his son stood before him in all his knightly glory. Silently they embraced, mounted their horses, and headed for the tournament grounds.

The stadium for the event was the grandest ever built. Never had there been such a huge congregation of lords and ladies in the history of England. The stands surrounded a great meadow, swept clean of all snow, with the combatants' tents at either end. In the central place of honor sat the archbishop. Patiently, he greeted each king and noble as they came forth to kiss his hand. "I should do this more often," he chuckled to himself.

The first event was the mock battle, or *mêlée*. The contestants were divided into two teams—the Reds and the Greens. Sir Kay was with the Reds, who gathered at the southern end of the field, while their opponents took the north. They all readied their lances and brought down their helmet visors in anticipation of combat. Everyone looked to the archbishop for a signal. Slowly, he raised his handkerchief, paused, and let it flutter to the ground. From either end of the field, the thunder of thousands of horse hooves rolled forward, shaking the earth, rattling the stands—louder and louder until a terrifying crash of metal split the air. A shower of splintered lances rained down in all directions. The audience gasped, and a few ladies fainted. Nothing had prepared them for this scale of violence.

Sir Kay performed admirably, for he charged ahead of his teammates and unseated two of the Greens. He was already winning accolades as he wheeled his charger around to aid a fellow Red.

"Sword. Sword. Where did I put that *sword?*" he muttered, desperately searching through the chests and bags. But to no avail.

How could this happen? he thought. Kay without a sword . . . and the whole world watching!

He paced back and forth, and then a thought struck him: Kay will *not* be without a sword today. I know where I can get one!

A few minutes later, he trotted into the churchyard where the sword in the anvil stood on the marble block. There wasn't a guard in sight—even they had gone to the tourney. Quietly, he brought his pony up to the stone and tugged on the reins.

"Okay, Blaze. . . . We'll just see if this sword can be unstuck," he whispered. He stretched out his arm until his fingers touched the hilt.

"Hey, it's looser than I thought. . . . Steady, Blaze! Steady, boy!" As the pony stepped back a few paces, the sword glided out of the anvil's grip, unbalancing Arthur. He regained his seat and looked down in wonder at the mighty blade in his hand.

"This isn't just *any* sword. . . . Perhaps it's something the church provides for needy strangers. Yes, that must be it! Well, I'll return it after the tournament. Someone else may need it. Thank you, sword, for saving me," he said, pressing its cross to his lips. "Wait until Kay sees this!"

He flung his cloak around the great sword and drove his little horse back to the tournament with lightning speed.

By now, Sir Kay had dismounted and was rather chafed.

"Arthur, where have you been?" he shouted. "You . . ."

He caught himself as Arthur dropped to one knee and opened the cloak.

"Your sword, my lord," Arthur said confidently. But his smile quickly disappeared when he saw Sir Kay's reaction. Frozen in place, his face white as milk, Sir Kay stared at the sword. Finally, he spoke.

"Where did you get this?" he asked Arthur, although he knew the answer.

Arthur confessed that he had searched in vain for Sir Kay's sword and had borrowed this one instead.

"Get Father at once, and tell no one of this!" said Sir Kay sternly.

Arthur thought he must be in terrible trouble. Surely he could return the sword without his father knowing. Why did Father have to be told? Nevertheless, he obeyed his brother and returned quickly with Sir Ector.

Sir Kay closed the curtains of the tent and opened the cloak, revealing the sword to his father.

Sir Ector gasped when he saw it. "How can this be?"

"Father, I am in possession of this sword," said Sir Kay nervously. "That is what matters. Therefore, I must be king of all Britain."

"But how came you by it, son?" asked Sir Ector.

"Well, sire, I needed a sword . . . and we couldn't find mine . . . so, I decided to use this one!" said Sir Kay. Beads of sweat formed on his brow.

"Very well, lad. You drew it out of the stone. I want to see you put it back. Let's go," said Sir Ector.

"But *I have the sword!*" said Sir Kay. "Isn't that enough?"

"No," replied Sir Ector, as he mounted his horse and headed toward the cathedral. Arthur rode close behind and, ever so slowly, Sir Kay mounted and followed.

The churchyard was still deserted when the three arrived. "Put the sword back in the anvil," said Sir Ector bluntly. "I must see it."

"Father, I . . ."

"Just do it, Kay, and you shall be king. If that's what you want." Sir Kay climbed onto the block. Sweat was now pouring off him. He raised the mighty sword over his head and plunged it downward. But the sharp point skidded across the surface of the anvil, causing Sir Kay to fall headfirst off the block.

"Now, son, tell me. How came you by this sword?" asked Sir Ector again.

"Arthur brought it to me," said Sir Kay, dusting himself off. "He *lost* my other one."

Suddenly a fear gripped Sir Ector's heart. "Arthur, my boy," he said quietly, "will you try it for us?"

"Certainly, Father," said Arthur, "but do we have to tell anyone about this? Can't we just . . ."

"Son, please," said Sir Ector solemnly. "If you can put the sword in that anvil, please do so now."

With a pounding heart, the lad took the sword from Sir Kay's hand and climbed slowly onto the block of marble. Raising it with both hands over his head, he thrust it downward, through the anvil, burying the point deep within the stone. Effortlessly he pulled it out again, glanced at his stunned father, and shoved the sword into the stone, even deeper this time.

Sir Ector shrieked and sank to his knees. His mouth moved, but no words came out. He put his hands together as in prayer. Silently, Sir Kay knelt and did the same.

"Father! What are you doing?" cried Arthur, leaping down from the stone. "Please! Get up! Get up! I don't understand!"

"Now I know!" sputtered Sir Ector, choking back tears. "Now I know who you are!"

"I'm your son, Father!" said the bewildered lad, crouching down by his father and putting his head to Sir Ector's chest.

After a few deep breaths, Sir Ector regained his composure. He smiled sadly down at Arthur and stroked his head.

"Fate would have it otherwise, my boy. Look there behind you." He pointed to the gold lettering on the marble block, which stated the purpose of the sword and the anvil.

Arthur sat in silence and stared at the words in the marble.

"Although you were adopted, I've loved you like my own child, Arthur," said Sir Ector softly. "But now I realize you have the blood of kings in you. To discover your birthright is the true reason we came to London. You are now our king and we your faithful servants."

At this, Arthur broke into tears. "I don't want to be king. Not if it means losing my father!" he sobbed.

"You have a great destiny before you, Arthur. There's no use avoiding it," said Sir Ector.

Arthur wiped his eyes with his sleeve. He straightened up so he could look Sir Ector in the eyes. A few minutes passed.

"Very well," Arthur finally said slowly. "Whatever my destiny may be, I am willing to accept it. But I still need you with me."

"Then so it shall be, lad. So it shall be," said Sir Ector.

They sat quietly for a time, comforting each other, until they felt another presence. From across the yard a hooded figure quietly floated into the fading light of the winter afternoon and knelt down beside them.

"Merlin," said Sir Ector, bowing his head to the famous enchanter.

"I've been waiting for you, Arthur," said the wizard.

"You know me, my lord?" asked Arthur.

"I put you in this good man's care many years ago and have kept an eye on you ever since."

"How did you do that, sire? We live far from here."

"Oh, I have my ways," replied Merlin. "But you still managed to surprise me. The sword-pulling contest isn't until tomorrow, and you pulled it out today!" he said with a chuckle.

"But what is to become of me now?" asked Arthur.

"Well, let us start with tomorrow," replied the old sorcerer. "We must still have the contest to prove to the world that you are the rightful heir. I will come for you when the time is right."

"But after that, sire, what is my future?" asked the boy.

Merlin weighed this question carefully. He wasn't at all sure whether the boy was prepared for his answer. Finally, he spoke. "I can tell you only what my powers suggest—and they point to greatness. Greatness surrounds you like a golden cloak. Your achievements could inspire humankind for centuries to come. But you alone can fulfill this destiny and then only if you wish it. You own your future. You alone."

Arthur breathed deeply and cast his eyes downward. He thought of all the good-byes he would have to say. He thought of his fishing hole, and the birds that ate seeds from his hand. He thought of the deer that came when he called them.

"What time tomorrow, sire?" he asked.

"After all have tried and failed, whenever that may be," replied Merlin.

"I will be ready, sire," said Arthur. Then he rose, bade Merlin farewell, and silently returned to his tent.

On Christmas morning, the archbishop said mass for the largest gathering he had seen in years. The grounds surrounding the cathedral were also filled—with those seeking to make history or watch it being made. As soon as the service ended, those who wished to try for the throne formed a line next to the marble block.

Leading the line was King Urien of Gore, husband to Margaise, Uther-Pendragon's adoptive daughter. Ever since the high king's death, Urien had claimed loudly that he was the rightful heir. Indeed, he took his position on the marble block with a great sense of authority and gave the sword a confident tug, then another, and another. Urien was sweating and yanking furiously when finally asked to step down.

Next came King Lot of Orkney, husband to Morgan le

Fay. King Lot felt certain that his wife's magical powers would assure his victory. But pull and tug as he might, he couldn't move the sword. After that, King Mark of Cornwall, King Leodegrance of Cameliard, and King Ryence of North Wales all took their place on the stone—and failed. The dukes of Winchester, Colchester, Worcester, and Hamcester did not fare any better. Some thought the longer they waited, the looser the sword would become, thereby improving their chances. But this wasn't the case, for the sword never budged, not even slightly. Kings, dukes, earls, counts, and knights all left that marble block empty-handed. Finally, as the day waned and the line neared its end, the crowd grew impatient for a winner. Merlin went for Arthur.

Sir Ector and Sir Kay opened the curtains of their tent when they saw Merlin approaching.

"Your hour has come, my lord," said the old wizard to Arthur, who was standing alone in the center of the tent. Silently, the boy walked forth as one in a dream.

The crowd made way for them as they entered, for Merlin was still revered by all. But who could these other people be? Especially that young blond lad dressed all in red. What was he doing here?

Merlin brought Arthur before the archbishop and bowed deeply. Arthur dropped to one knee.

"My lord," said Merlin, "I present to you a most worthy candidate for this contest. Has he your permission to attempt to pull yonder sword from the stone?"

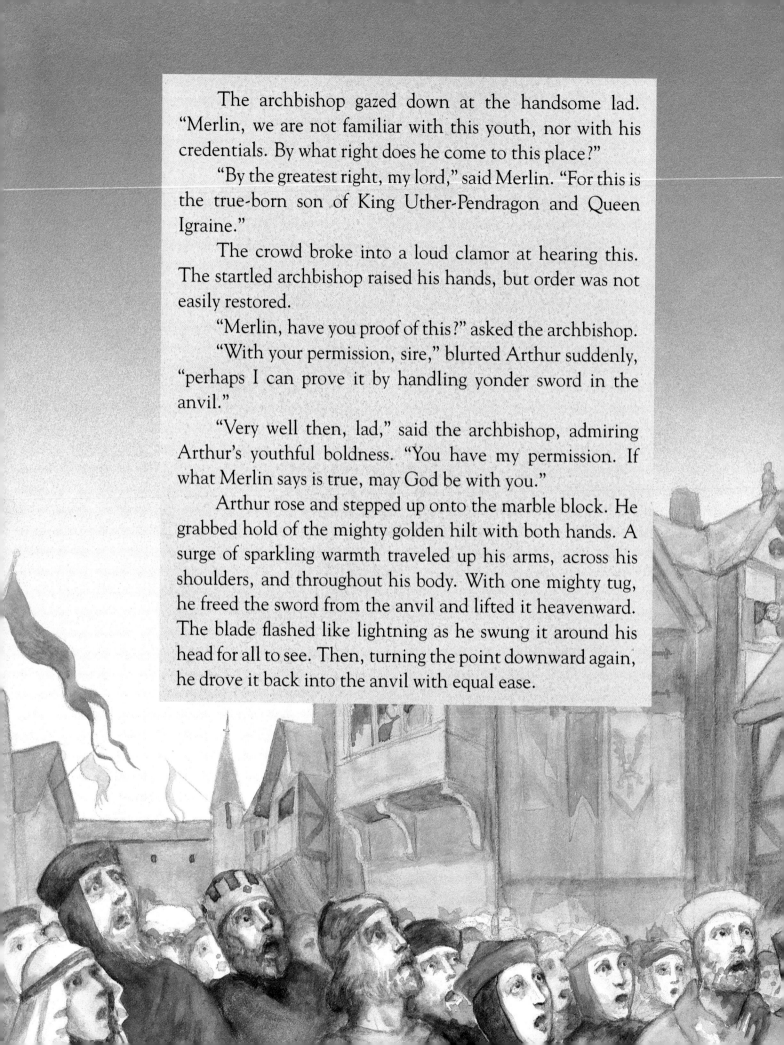

The archbishop gazed down at the handsome lad. "Merlin, we are not familiar with this youth, nor with his credentials. By what right does he come to this place?"

"By the greatest right, my lord," said Merlin. "For this is the true-born son of King Uther-Pendragon and Queen Igraine."

The crowd broke into a loud clamor at hearing this. The startled archbishop raised his hands, but order was not easily restored.

"Merlin, have you proof of this?" asked the archbishop.

"With your permission, sire," blurted Arthur suddenly, "perhaps I can prove it by handling yonder sword in the anvil."

"Very well then, lad," said the archbishop, admiring Arthur's youthful boldness. "You have my permission. If what Merlin says is true, may God be with you."

Arthur rose and stepped up onto the marble block. He grabbed hold of the mighty golden hilt with both hands. A surge of sparkling warmth traveled up his arms, across his shoulders, and throughout his body. With one mighty tug, he freed the sword from the anvil and lifted it heavenward. The blade flashed like lightning as he swung it around his head for all to see. Then, turning the point downward again, he drove it back into the anvil with equal ease.

The entire gathering stood dumbstruck for a long moment, trying to comprehend what they had just seen. Arthur looked about for reassurance. He looked to Sir Ector, then Merlin, and then the archbishop. They all simply stared at him, with eyes wide in amazement. A child giggled and clapped his hands in glee, then so did another, and another. Cheers began to ring out as people found their voices again. Suddenly, a thunder of shouting and clapping rose up around Arthur. Amidst the tumult, he closed his eyes and whispered, "Thank you, Father."

Then he grabbed the sword's hilt for a second time and withdrew it. As he brought it above his head, a thousand swords throughout the crowd were raised in solidarity. Arthur drove the sword back into the anvil and pulled it out once again. This time, as he lifted the great blade to the sky, more swords and halberds were raised, along with brooms, rakes, and walking sticks, as counts and common folk alike saluted their newfound king.

Not everyone was overjoyed at this turn of events, however. Although all had seen the miracle performed, several kings and dukes were unwilling to recognize Arthur's right to the throne. Loudest among the grumblers were King Lot and King Urien, Arthur's brothers-in-law. "How dare this beardless, unknown country boy think he can be made high king to rule over us!" they said. "Obviously, Merlin is using the boy to promote himself!"

But these malcontents gained no support from those around them and were quickly shouted down. So they gathered themselves together and stormed away in a huff of indignation.

To everyone else, the day belonged to Arthur. All the other kings and nobles rushed forth to show their acceptance, for they trusted Merlin and were grateful to have a leader at last. They hoisted the young king-to-be above their heads to parade him through the streets of London.

As the noisy procession flowed out of the churchyard, the archbishop hobbled over to Merlin to offer congratulations for a successful plan.

"Thank you, my lord, but I think we are not yet finished," said the wizard.

The archbishop looked puzzled.

"I fear that King Lot and King Urien and those other discontented souls will leave us no peace until they have another chance at the sword," continued Merlin. "We must offer them a new trial on New Year's Day."

And so they did. But again, no one could budge the sword but Arthur. These same troublesome kings and dukes still refused to acknowledge his victory, though. So another trial took place on Candlemas, and yet another on Easter.

By now, the people had grown impatient, for they had believed in Arthur all along and had grown to love him. The idea of having a fresh young king inspired hope and optimism. The world suddenly felt young again.

Finally, after the trial held on Pentecost, they cried out, "Enough! Arthur has proven himself five times now! We will have him for our king—and no other!"

The archbishop and Merlin agreed. There was proof beyond dispute at this point. So the coronation was set for May Day in the great cathedral of London.

Upon arriving that morning, Arthur stepped up on the block and pulled the sword from the anvil for the last time. With the blade pointing heavenward, he entered the church, walked solemnly down the central aisle, and laid the sword upon the altar. The archbishop administered the holy sacraments and finally placed the crown upon Arthur's head.

Ten thousand cheers burst forth as the young king emerged from the cathedral. At Merlin's suggestion, Arthur stepped up on the marble block to speak to the people. A hush fell over the masses as he raised his hands to address them.

"People of Britain, we are now one. And so shall we remain as long as there is a breath in my body. My faith in your courage and wisdom is boundless. I ask now for your faith in me. In your trust I shall find my strength. For your good I dedicate my life. May this sword lead us to our destiny."

AFTERWORD

Few stories have captured the imagination of people around the world as have the legends of King Arthur and his Round Table. Believed to have grown out of the exploits of a sixth-century British military leader, these tales of magic, romance, and chivalry have become a symbol of what we aspire to as a society.

The first written record concerning King Arthur dates back to a twelfth-century manuscript by Sir Geoffrey of Monmouth. His *History of the Kings of Britain* presented Arthur, Merlin, and the Round Table as a factual part of British history. But it was Sir Thomas Malory's epic collection of tales about King Arthur, written in 1469–70 and published by the great British printer William Caxton in 1485 under the title *Morte Darthur*, that established the Arthurian legends as a cornerstone of British folklore. *Morte Darthur*—one of the first books ever printed in Britain—quickly proved immensely popular and was reprinted several times over the next century.

As the Renaissance and Enlightenment—the great ages of scientific discovery and learning throughout Europe—continued, the popularity of the Arthurian legends waned. Between 1634 and 1816, no editions of King Arthur's adventures were published in English. But with the explosion of children's books in the nineteenth century, the stories of King Arthur were revived and established themselves firmly as childhood favorites.

As the epic became more popular, many of the legends began to take on lives of their own. One of the most popular legends has always been the story of how the young Arthur discovered his heritage and came to be king of all England. Referred to as "The Sword in the Stone" since the end of the nineteenth century, this tale of an innocent country lad's magical rise to kingship continues to enchant people of all ages.

Many famous children's book writers—among them Howard Pyle, Sidney Lanier, T. H. White, and Rosemary Sutcliff—have retold the legends of King Arthur in their own unique way. But all these versions are for older children; rarely have the legends been fashioned for younger readers and listeners.

In this new retelling of "The Sword in the Stone," Hudson Talbott captures all the romance and excitement of the classic legend in a story that young listeners can follow easily and so be transported back through time to the very start of the magical legends of King Arthur.

—Peter Glassman